Shut It!

by

Pete Johnson

You do not need to read this page –
just get on with the book!

First published in 2009 in Great Britain by
Barrington Stoke Ltd
18 Walker St, Edinburgh, EH3 7LP

www.barringtonstoke.co.uk

ISBN: 978-1-84299-690-4

Printed in Great Britain by Bell & Bain Ltd

AUTHOR ID

Name: Pete Johnson

Likes: Being on holiday, chocolate Easter eggs, clear blue skies, black and white films.

Dislikes: Grey, cold mornings, January, bossy people, the end of a holiday, orange juice.

3 words that best describe me:
Humorous, imaginative, loyal.

A secret not many people know:
I used to be a regular sleep walker. Once I sleep-walked right out of my house and down the road. Luckily, I was wearing pyjamas!

This story is dedicated to my two nephews: Harry and Adam.
With grateful thanks for all their help and advice!

Contents

Chapter 1
Two Massive Fights

I wish I could make my brother Andy vanish. I wish I could say a spell that made him vanish for ever. All right, not for ever. Too harsh. Just until I've grown up – and left home.

And I really wouldn't miss Andy. Not for one second. All he and I do is argue about everything.

For a start – take last Saturday morning. Mum's about to drive into town with Andy and me – I'm Ben, by the way. We're going shopping. Andy gets in the car and sits in the front.

"Hey, what are you doing?" I shout.

"I'm sitting in a car, Ben," he replies. "People do it a lot these days."

"But it's my turn to sit in the front," I say.

"No, it isn't," snarls Andy.

"Yes, it is, you sat there last Saturday," I cry.

"But I'm the oldest," says Andy.

"That's got nothing to do with it," I say. "Now, move."

"No, I'm staying here," says Andy.

Then, of course, I try and pull Andy out of the front seat. This is difficult – he's much bigger than me.

Then Mum comes out to the car. We're still pushing and yelling at each other. I try and tell her what's happened but she puts her hands over her ears and says, "I haven't got time for this. No one sits in the front. You can both sit in the back."

"But that's not fair," I say. "It's my turn."

"I don't care whose turn it is," says Mum. "No one's sitting in the front today."

So Andy and I squash into the back. Then we have another fight.

"Hey, stop looking out of my window," I say. "Look out of your own."

"I'll do what I want," says Andy. He leans over me and pushes me so he can look out of the window.

So I punch him. He yells out. And Mum stops the car. She yells a bit too. And neither Andy or me are allowed to say a word for the rest of the journey.

But Andy and I have another massive fight later. This time it's about the TV remote.

Andy and I don't have TVs in our bedrooms. And there's only one telly downstairs. So what does Andy do? He hides the TV remote so no one can ever switch on the TV downstairs except him. And then he can pick which programmes we watch.

"Why are you acting as if you're in charge of the remote?" I say.

"Because I am," he replies.

"That's total rubbish," I yell and I run off to get Mum, but she's not really interested. She hardly ever watches TV anyway and she says, "Oh, just sort it out."

But I can't sort out anything with Andy. He's always been difficult, but since Dad left he's been much worse. Now Andy thinks he can boss me about when he wants. He's 13 and a half. I'm 12. That's not much older at all, is it? How does that give him the right to tell me what to do?

The trouble is he looks much older than me. He's big and taller than many of our teachers already. And he's started to shave. He says it's every day, but I know it's not. I'm still not that tall yet. And I'm a bit skinny. Sometimes I get teased at school because of that. But I'm standing up for myself more and more.

And I think I'm cool. Until one night, something truly terrible happens.

I'd just got a girlfriend – my first one ever. Her name's Tara and she's new in my class at school. Every boy in the school fancies her. I thought she'd go out with someone years older than me.

But I heard she liked me. So I asked her out. I thought she'd say no. Everyone else thought so too. But she didn't, she said yes. An incredible **yes**.

We went to the cinema and then I went round to her house for tea. Her mum and dad were pretty cool with me. Tara told me later that her parents really liked me. It was all going so brilliantly – she even laughed at all my jokes.

And so on Thursday night Tara's coming to my house. I picked that night because Andy's out at football on Thursdays.

Football's the only thing he's any good at. But at the last minute his football gets cancelled so Andy will be at home after all.

Mum says, "Now don't worry. Andy won't spoil this for you, I promise. You'll have a great evening."

And I believe Mum, don't I?

Big, big mistake.

Chapter 2
A Terrible Night

It's Thursday night. Tara arrives at six o'clock. I open the door and she grins at me. She looks so happy. Then she meets Mum. And right away I know Mum likes her.

Mum treats us as if we're grown-ups. She tells us to sit in the lounge. The food will be ready soon. She brings in peanuts and drinks. And we sit there sipping our drinks, feeling quite grown-up.

I can hear Andy thumping about upstairs. He sounds cross. This makes me very happy. I put on some music, loud so we can't hear Andy stamping about. Mum always has a go at me when I have the music up loud. But today she doesn't say a word.

Tara starts telling me what music she likes. And it's the same as me. What about that? No wonder my stomach goes all wobbly. What a perfect evening this is.

And then Andy storms into the room. "Tara," I start to say, "you may have seen this boy at school. This is my ..."

But Andy doesn't let me finish my sentence. "You're not going out with him, are you?" he shouts.

Tara nods.

Andy laughs as if he'd just heard the funniest joke in the world.

"I should have told you about my brother," I sighed, "he's totally mad."

Andy goes on laughing then he lands on a chair across from us. He sits down with a big thump and everything in the room seems to shake. Then he folds his arms and tells us, "This music is total rubbish."

"Tara and I really like it," I reply.

"No taste," Andy murmurs, and slouches back in his chair. I try to talk to Tara, but it's difficult because Andy's like some great wart-hog snorting about, right in front of us.

And then Andy starts to wave his hands about as if he's a policeman telling cars where to go. Is he doing his keep-fit exercises or freaking out to the music? I glare at him. But he hisses back at me, "Put your arm around her, you moron. Go on, get stuck in."

Tara can hear every word Andy says. And I know he only wants to embarrass me. I feel my face start to turn red. But then Tara reaches out and grabs my hand. And we sit there holding hands. Andy doesn't like this at all. He grunts and gets up and leaves.

"One nil – to us!" I murmur. But then we hear him outside the door making silly kissing noises. I switch the music up even louder.

Then Mum comes in. "We're all ready for you," she says, with a big smile.

We go into the kitchen. The table is all set up as if it's Christmas. "Now tuck in and enjoy," says Mum.

Andy doesn't say much. He's too busy eating. I've never seen him so hungry.

Later Mum gets out some photos to show Tara. Of course there's one of me as a baby, and on my first day at school. But they aren't too bad.

But then Andy gets out another photo of me. It's my school photo from about six months ago. And at the time I had the most terrible zits you've ever seen. They were all over my face. I was like Zit Man.

And the photo shows the zits in their full horror. I begin to shake with panic. Tara hasn't ever seen me look like that. Will the photo put her off me? Most of the spots have gone now. But that photo makes me look like a monster from *Dr Who*.

I push the photo onto the floor. Andy picks it up, grins and then he's gone.

"I think that's enough photos," I say.

Then Mum says, "You and Tara, go back into the lounge." Mum shouts up the stairs,

"Andy – you can help me stack the dishwasher."

"It's not my turn," Andy begins to shout back. But then he looks downstairs and sees Mum's face. He thumps back down.

Tara and I go into the lounge. But I feel suddenly shy with her, and awkward. She's not saying anything either. Should I say something about that terrible photo? I'm too ashamed. We sit down, and at first I don't notice what is on the table. It's Tara who sees it first. She goes, "Oh," in a shocked voice.

And then I see it too. Right in the middle of the table is a huge bottle of zit cream. It seems to tower over us. Everything else in the room shrinks.

It wasn't there before. Andy must have dug it out of my cupboard and put it there. Of all the mean nasty things to do. All I can do is look at it in shock ... and then Andy comes in. He looks dead pleased with himself.

"Did you put that zit cream here?" I demand.

"Never use the stuff," said Andy, "but then I don't get spots like you. You get them something rotten. It is yours, isn't it?"

"Look, it really doesn't matter," Tara says and then she laughs. "I think it's quite funny really."

I'm so angry I turn on her. "Funny," I yell. "There's nothing funny about it!"

She looks shocked now.

"Don't have a go at her," says Andy.

"I'm not having a go," I shout.

"Yes you are," says Andy. "You're being very rude to her."

"You're the rude one. You brought this zit cream down here," I say.

"Oh, that – it's only a joke," he says. "That's the trouble with your boyfriend, isn't it?" he says as he turns to Tara. "He can't take a joke."

"A joke!" I yell and I hurl the bottle at him.

Andy gets ready to punch me just as Mum comes in. "Well, how are we in here?" she asks.

Andy and I start shouting together about what's happened. But then a third voice starts up. "I'd like to go home now."

Andy and I shut up at once. Tara carries on. "I'll just call my dad," she says and starts

15

whispering into her mobile. Then she thanks Mum for the "lovely meal," and says good-bye to me. That "Good-bye" sounds like it's for ever. And she doesn't look at me either.

I'm in bits but I try to look calm. "Well, see you soon then, Tara," I say. "I mean, I'll see you at school of course, but maybe we could meet up again ... sometime." My voice falls away and Tara doesn't say a word. Then her dad's car pulls up and she runs out of the house.

"What was the matter with that poor girl?" asks Mum.

"Ben told her off for laughing," says Andy.

"No I didn't ... it was you." Then I pick up the zit cream from the floor and tell Mum what Andy did.

"Oh, that's a nasty thing to do," Mum says to Andy.

This makes Andy laugh even more and then he says, "I was only messing about, that's all."

"No, you weren't," I say. "You really don't want me to have a girlfriend, do you?"

Andy turns away from me.

"Just because you're so ugly no girl would ever look at you," I shout.

"That's all you know, spotty," begins Andy.

"That's enough," says Mum.

But then Andy hisses. "Who's been dumped ... Do you think she'll tell everyone how you told her off for laughing?"

"Shut it!" I scream.

"I won't tell you again," cries Mum. "Both of you be quiet."

"But it's all his fault," I cry.

"You're both at fault," Mum says.

"No, we're not," I say. "It's all him. It's all his fault – it always is. But you can never see that." And then I stomp upstairs.

I'm so angry I can't sit still. Then I think of Tara – and how she didn't even look at me when she left. And I feel more than a bit sick.

Downstairs I can hear Mum and Andy talking. Andy will be getting round Mum as always.

I know tomorrow will be terrible. There'll be Andy looking at me at breakfast. He'll be really pleased with himself and making more stupid comments. Then Mum will tell me off for getting angry.

As for school – Andy'll tell everyone about me being dumped. Soon they'll all be whispering about it. I still can't believe it.

Tara and I are finished – because of one bottle of spot cream; and an evil brother.

I fall asleep at last. It's about four o'clock. And I wake up again just after six o'clock. Outside it's raining. This is going to be a really horrible day.

And then suddenly I have an idea. It's so brilliant it shocks me. I sit up in bed.

Yes, that's what I will do.

Chapter 3
I Give Up Talking

I'm going to do something which will amaze everyone.

I'm not going to say one single word for a whole month. I shall stay totally silent.

I creep downstairs and find some paper. I'll write down anything I need to say.

I write out my first bit of paper. It says –
I've given up talking for a month. This is

because I have a rubbish life – and a really rubbish brother.

I look at what I've written – and smile. All at once I'm looking forward to today. At breakfast Andy's the first one down, as usual. And he's already shovelling down his Coco Pops when he sees me. He grins and I smile back. That gives him a shock.

"I don't know what you're looking so happy about," he says.

I just carry on smiling.

Andy looks at me. He knows I'm up to something. Then Mum hurries in. "I'd like a day with no shouting for once. Can you two do that?"

I smile and nod. Mum is about to get a whole month of not hearing me at all.

Andy looks at me. "Why do you keep smiling all the time?"

I show them what I've written. Andy reads it and bursts out laughing, but in a loud, over-the-top way. "That's the best news I've heard for years. You couldn't make it a year, could you?"

But Mum looks worried. "What is this all about?"

I point at Andy. He shows her my piece of paper.

She frowns. "You can't stop talking – at school."

I start writing fast and then hold up another bit of paper – **at school people get into trouble for talking. Teachers want you to be quiet.**

Mum still looks puzzled. But Andy jumps up. "If he wants to be stupid, let him," he says. Then quick as a flash he's gone.

"I think he's upset," Mum says, "about you writing that he's a rubbish brother."

I just stare at her. Sometimes my mum amazes me. She thinks Andy's upset. But what about me? Mum looks as if she wants to say something else – but she doesn't.

On the way to school I buy some extra pads of paper. I have a feeling I'll need them today.

I don't want to see Tara in class. But luckily she's not in there. Mr Lewis, our form teacher stomps in. He's a small man with a beard and a very bad temper. "Right, silence, everyone while I take the register," he says.

Everyone shuts up at once. No one wants to get Mr Lewis mad.

He snaps out the names and everyone calls out, "Yes, sir," until he reaches me. I hold up a piece of paper which says **yes, sir**. But Mr Lewis doesn't see it so I get up and walk over to his desk.

"Ben Cross," he calls again.

Then he does see me standing in front of him. I point at the paper that says **yes, sir** and give a polite smile.

Mr Lewis must be a slow reader because he stares at the paper for nearly a minute without saying anything. "What's this all about?" he says at last and looks hard at me.

I hold up the first bit of paper which I wrote out this morning. The one that explains everything – about my rubbish life and my rubbish brother. He stares at it and some of the boys in my form begin to laugh rather loudly.

"I want everyone in this room to be silent," roars Mr Lewis. Then he turns to me "Except you, Ben. You must start talking now."

I write – **sorry, I can't do that.**

"How dare you come into my classroom and not talk," says Mr Lewis. "You are being very rude indeed."

I write – **how can I be rude when I haven't said a single word?**

"Oh, sit down and stop wasting my time," Mr Lewis grunts. Then he adds, "I'm sure you'll be talking by break time."

Chapter 4
Everything Changes

After registration, everyone's asking me questions. Then a boy stands on my feet because he wants me to yell out. But I just hold up some paper. I've written **ouch** on it. The boy laughs and goes away.

Then a girl says, "If you talk, I'll give you ten pounds." I shake my head. The girl looks amazed. But I don't think she'd really have given me ten pounds.

The next lesson is Maths. And the teacher doesn't even notice I've stopped talking, she's so busy talking herself. In History, I get asked a question. I know the answer so I quickly write it down on a piece of paper.

The History teacher stops and stares. "Ben's not talking for a whole month," says a girl.

"Now what's the chance of the rest of you following Ben's example," grins the teacher, "because the peace in this room would be wonderful."

The History teacher doesn't say anything else to me. But at the end of the lesson he says. "If ever you want to talk about anything ..."

I smile and shake my head.

"Well, I'm a good listener," he smiles at me and looks at my bits of paper, "and a very keen reader too." Then he calls as I walk out of the class, "I hope you feel better soon," as if I've been ill.

It's lunch-time now and I'm on the way to the dinner hall. But I can't get there. Out on the playground almost half the school edges round me. They've all heard about my protest – and they want to ask me about it. Funny, really, it's when you stop talking that everyone wants to talk to you.

In the middle of the crowd is Tara. She was late to school this morning and hasn't even tried to speak to me. Still, what would she say? "Thanks for a truly terrible evening. You're dumped." I really don't want to hear her say that. In fact, I can hardly look at her.

Andy's there too, his face red and angry because of all the fuss I'm getting. Everyone's talking about me today.

28

Then this gang of boys rush over to me and yell, "Freak." "Wuss." "Weirdo." "Loser." They get louder and ruder. But it's a funny thing, I don't care. Once you've given up using words, what people say hardly bothers you.

"Come on, say something," yell the boys. I just look at them with a little smile on my face. The boys shout out even ruder words.

But I still don't react.

Then Carl, who's in Year Ten, comes over and says, "Big respect for what you're doing, Ben. Why should we have to talk – if we don't want to? You're fighting for our right to be quiet, aren't you?"

I nod my head – he's right but I'd never thought of that before.

"You're a true rebel," Carl goes on. Other Year Ten boys start patting me on the back then. And then Carl says. "This might sound a little mad but could I write about you in the school magazine? Can I ask you some questions? Do an interview?"

No one from my class has ever been in the school magazine before. They can't believe what's going on.

At lunch break I go to this small office which the school newspaper can use. I've never even spoken to Carl before. Now he can't stop asking me questions. And he reads out the answers I write.

"You're turning into a bit of a hero?" he says.

Then he tells me his cousin is doing work experience for the local paper. "He's looking for a really big story ... could he come and do an interview with you?"

I nod my head.

"It might be best if he comes to your house," says Carl. I write down my address.

Then I send Tara a text. It's very short. It just says –

Im very very sorry

She doesn't text me back. And she ignores me all afternoon. But no one else does. People want to know how I got the idea of not talking. **It just came to me**, I write. One girl even says, "This could be the next big thing."

Suddenly I think about teenagers all over the country not talking – until their lives get better. And I'm their leader. I might even appear on the news. "Here he is, the leader of the new teenage craze called 'Shut it'."

You just stop talking – and see your life change.

In one single day I've become really popular. Everyone wants to know me now. It's incredible. And by the afternoon the teachers have stopped telling me off. In English, Miss Webb just says, "It's all right, Ben, I know you're not speaking today." She says this in such a soft, kind voice, it's a bit spooky.

Does she think I've gone mad? Oh, well, wait until she sees my picture in the local newspaper. I had a text saying a reporter is coming to my house at five o'clock. I'm very excited.

And I run out of the school and right into my brother.

Andy and I never leave school together. And if ever Mum picks us up, we wait at different places outside the school.

But today, Andy is waiting for me with four of his mates. They all tower over me.

"What have you been saying about me?" asks Andy.

I write **I haven't said a single word all day.**

Andy grabs the bit of paper and screws it up. "You've been telling everyone what a rubbish brother I am."

I start to write **well you are** ...

Andy grabs up that bit of paper too. "Start speaking now," he says, "or I'll beat you up."

Chapter 5
"Bring It On"

Andy and I argue all the time. But he's never beaten me up before.

"Come on, say something," he yells. He looks as if he's about to punch me. "Say something or you'll be sorry."

I get my bits of paper and write three words as big as I can –

BRING IT ON

I'm not a brave person, but just then I don't feel like me. I feel like I'm the leader of the "Shut it" craze. And I glare back at my brother.

There's a crowd of people gathering around us now. Any moment Andy's fist is going to swing towards me. He drops his head down as if he's a mad bull about to charge. I close my eyes and wait. But nothing happens. Then I hear Andy run off at a terrific speed. Even his mates are amazed. "Must have lost his bottle," they say. "Not like Andy to get scared."

Everyone is patting me on the back. "You really stood up to your brother," they say. But I'm puzzled. Why did Andy suddenly run off like that? When I get home I expect him to be there already. But he isn't. And Mum is waiting for me.

"I've had your school on the phone," she says. "They're worried about you not talking. How much longer are you going to do this?"

I write down **30 days.**

Mum groans. "This has got to stop right now. Do you understand?"

I nod. "Yes, I understand." Then I shake my head as well – to show I'll carry on for the 30 days.

Mum stares at me. "I know this is about last night. And Andy knows he went too far. I told him to say sorry to you. He said he was going to sort things out."

Well he hasn't, I write.

Mum says, "I don't know why he hasn't"

I know why. And I write **he's not sorry at all.**

Then I add – **the local paper is coming to interview me later**.

Mum is so shocked by this news she has to sit down. "Oh, this has gone too far," she groans.

Then the front door opens and in thumps Andy, looking fed up. "Andy," says Mum.

"What?" he snaps.

"Don't say 'what' in that rude voice," Mum says.

"Well, I won't say anything then – like him," he says and he points at me.

"Don't be silly," cries Mum. "I want you to say sorry to Ben for last night.

"Never," he almost shouts. "You'll have to throw me out of the house before I do that."

And he storms off.

Mum looks upset – and angry. "Come on, Ben," she says. "You know why Andy acted so badly last night, don't you?"

Because he's mean and selfish ...

I'm writing this but Mum puts her hands over the words and looks hard at me. "No. He was like that because he's jealous of you having a pretty girlfriend. Last night wasn't easy for him, you know."

I look at her. What *is* going on? How dare Mum try and make me feel sorry for Andy.

Then the doorbell rings.

It's the reporter come to interview me.

Chapter 6
A Surprise Visitor

The reporter looks young and keen.

"I'm Jim, Carl's cousin. And you're Ben from Carl's school?"

I nod firmly.

"The boy who isn't going to talk for a month ..."

I nod again.

"Well look, could I do an interview with you?"

I'm writing **yes of course**, when Mum comes up behind me ...

"Hello, I'm Ben's mum and I'm sorry but I'm not very happy about this interview. I feel it's just leading Ben on in something very silly."

"Well, can I just ask your son a few questions, please?" Jim asks Mum.

"No," Mum says firmly. "No questions at all. Sorry you've wasted your time."

But when Mum isn't looking I show Jim another note. **I'll meet you outside in about 10 minutes.**

I can't miss out on that interview. This is my chance to make "Shut it" world famous.

Then Mum calls Andy downstairs. He thumps into the kitchen and glares at me.

Andy says, "Ben's starting to really stress me out. He's such a show-off ... not talking."

"Well, I agree," says Mum. "Not talking is always silly. After all, talking is how we sort things out. But," and she looks hard at Andy. "You should say sorry to your brother for last night."

So Andy puts on this silly high voice. "Oh, wonderful brother of mine, I'm deeply, truly sorry for my very bad actions. Can you please forgive me?"

I long to just shout back at him. Writing everything down takes ages. But instead, I scribble **don't waste your breath. I know you don't mean it.**

Andy reads what I've written and then he says, "Too right, I don't. Just get over yourself. You're nothing special."

"That's enough," Mum almost screams. "What is the matter with both of you?"

"If you want to know," says Andy, "I think it's very bad manners never to answer people. But do you tell him off? Oh, no, he can get away with it, because he's Mr Perfect."

"Don't be silly," says Mum.

"You always think he is," snaps Andy.

"I've told Ben that not talking is ..."

"Totally sad," Andy butts in.

"And I'm asking Ben to start talking again now," goes on Mum.

Then she waits. But I just frown and look away from her. I know I'm upsetting Mum, and that makes me feel bad. But I can't give up my protest now. Nothing has changed. Andy's still as totally annoying as ever.

And then the doorbell rings. "I expect that's the reporter again," says Mum. "I'll deal with him. You two don't move. This is going to be sorted out right now." She walks off. Andy and I are on our own.

We don't say or write a single word to each other. There's just this heavy, deep silence. Then Mum returns. "There's someone who wants to have a word with you, Ben. It's Tara."

That's a shock all right. I don't look at Andy or Mum. Instead, my heart thumps. I go into the hall-way. Tara's not smiling. I know she's going to dump me. I'm glad at least she didn't do it at school.

"I've got something to say to you," she says.

I swallow hard. Should I ask her to give me another chance and say how much I like her? And then I see something very odd.

She's holding up a card. It says – *I'm very sorry too*.

I grin at her and then start to write. **But it's really my fault** ... only she stops me.

"Let's just forget last night," she says.

I nod.

"And would you say thank you to your brother for his text?"

"My brother sent you a text?" The words just burst out of my mouth.

Then Tara looks astonished too. "You're talking again."

"Yes," I say as if I'm in a dream. "It's just – you said my brother sent you a text."

"That's right. Andy texted me to say sorry for what he'd done. He said it was his fault that everything went wrong. He was just trying to wind you up."

"My brother wrote that." I shake my head. "That's the weirdest thing I've ever heard." But then I remember Mum saying how Andy was upset after Tara came round.

"I think he just wanted to tease you," said Tara. "And things got out of control. Anyway, the reason I came round was ... well, how about if we meet up in the park."

"Yeah, of course," I say.

"In about twenty minutes?" she goes on.

"Perfect," I reply.

"And will you still be talking then?"

I grin. "I think so, yes."

"Even better," she smiles back.

Then I go back into the kitchen. "Hello, everyone," I say.

Mum and Andy both spin round.

"Yes, I'm talking again. Er, Mum, could I have a word with Andy by himself, please?"

"Of course," says Mum. "Just remember you are brothers ..."

"See you, Mum," I cut in.

She leaves and Andy gives me an odd look. "I knew you couldn't stop talking for a month ... didn't even make one day," he says.

"It's because I miss chatting to you so much," I say. Then I say, "I could have killed you last night."

"I could kill you most nights," he murmurs.

"But, anyway, thanks for texting Tara."

"You see, I did sort it all out," says Andy.

"After you made it all go wrong in the first place."

He ignores this. "You didn't need to stop talking. You were just showing off, as normal. And then you told everyone you weren't talking because of me. That made me look a right idiot."

"You are," I reply.

Then Andy says. "And I never told a single person about what happened here last night."

That gives me a shock.

Andy goes on. "You thought I did – but then you always think the worst of me. So are you going to see her again?"

"Off to the park to meet her now," I say.

"She's too good for you," Andy says. "And no way will it last. No way."

"Cheers for that."

"Just try and not mess it up again," says Andy.

"All right, I'll try." I grin at him and I can't believe it when I see a smile sneak on to his face too.

I suppose there are worse brothers in the world than him. Somewhere.

I tell Mum where I'm going, then I'm off. As I walk out of the house I spot Jim, the reporter.

"Hello again," Jim says.

"Hi there," I reply.

He steps back in surprise. "But you're talking."

"I'm afraid so," I say.

"So what happened?" he asks.

"I had this massive shock – and the words just fell out of my mouth."

The reporter shakes his head. "That's a shame; my cousin said you were going to start a new craze called ... what was it?"

"'Shut it'," I say. I think about that for a moment and then say, "but I'm not sure I could've just written notes for a whole month. It really makes your hand hurt."

He gives a sigh. "Still, it would have been a great story."

"Yes," I agree, "but I think an even better story is waiting for me."

Jim looks puzzled but I don't explain. Instead, I race to the park – and Tara.

Barrington Stoke would like to thank all its readers for commenting on the manuscript before publication and in particular:

Christine Bilham
Josh Brannon
Freddie Burgoyne
Shannon Butcher
Hugo Cadman
D. Caldwell
Jordyn Campbell
Charlotte Clarke
Connor Cornell
Grace Crossley
Thomas Dadd
Tom Davies
Bonnie Dryschute
Cameron Fry
Sebastian Hayes

Sally Hopkins
Jeffrey Joubert
Harry Lester
Bobby Lindsay
Joseph Lonergan
Ryan Martin
Karen McCaffery
James Nuttall
Chris Shepherd
Jessica Stevens
Milo Samengo Turner
Ellie Wilkins
Demi Wilson
Wilhelm Würtemberg

Become a Consultant!

Would you like to give us feedback on our titles before they are published? Contact us at the email address below – we'd love to hear from you!

info@barringtonstoke.co.uk
www.barringtonstoke.co.uk

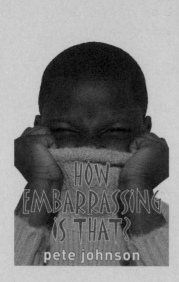

How Embarrassing is That?
by
Pete Johnson

Ruby knows who will win the contest for the most embarrassing parents. Her parents wear young clothes. They think they're her best mates. Her dad tells awful jokes. And now they're planning to sing in school assembly. They must be stopped – for good!

Desirable
by
Frank Cottrell Boyce

George is a loser. Then he starts using the aftershave that he got for his birthday. Suddenly all the girls are in love with him ... and that includes the teachers! George wanted to be popular. Now he's looking for somewhere to hide ...

You can order these books directly from our website at
www.barringtonstoke.co.uk

The Story of Matthew Buzzington
by
Andy Stanton

Who on earth is Matthew Buzzington, I hear you ask? Well, he's just a normal 10-year-old boy. But ... Matthew Buzzington can turn into a fly. Imagine that! It's just, that, well, he hasn't yet. But with robbers and flying pineapples out to get him – he needs to make his super-power work! Can he do it?

The Robbers
by
Josh Lacey

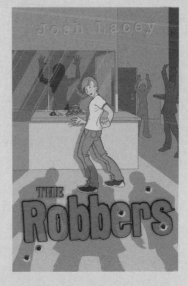

Peter thought it would be a normal Saturday at the bank.
But armed robbers have stormed in, taken everyone hostage – and now he's helping them to steal the cash. What the robbers don't know is that Peter will do anything to get his money back ...

You can order these books directly from our website at
www.barringtonstoke.co.uk